On Monday When It Rained

by Cherryl Kachenmeister
Photographs by Tom Berthiaume

Houghton Mifflin Company
Boston

For Maggie and Gracie
With thanks to Sebastian, Doris, Patricia

Library of Congress Cataloging-in-Publication Data

Kachenmeister, Cherryl.
    On Monday when it rained / Cherryl Kachenmeister; photographs by
Tom Berthiaume.
        p.   cm.
    Summary: A young boy describes, in text and photographs of his
facial expressions, the different emotions he feels each day.
    ISBN 0-395-51940-3
    [1. Emotions—Fiction.]   I. Berthiaume, Tom, ill.   II. Title.
PZ7. K1160n   1989   89-32361
[E]—dc20   CIP
                           AC

Printed in the United States of America

HOR 10 9 8 7 6 5 4 3

On Monday when it rained
my mother said I couldn't play outside.

I wanted to ride
my new red bike with the blue horn
to my friend Maggie's house.

I was…

Disappointed

On Tuesday when my grandma came to dinner
we had macaroni and cheese and chocolate milk.

I drank my chocolate milk real fast,
and right before we had the cookies for dessert
I burped out loud.

I was…

Embarrassed

On Wednesday when I went to pre-school
we drew pictures of big animals in a zoo.

My teacher, Laura, said
my elephant looked just like one
she saw at the zoo last summer.

I was…

Proud

On Thursday when I watched a movie
there was this one part where a big monster
ate a whole building.

My sister said that monsters aren't real,
but this one was green and had a long tail and scales
and it looked real to me.

I was…

Scared

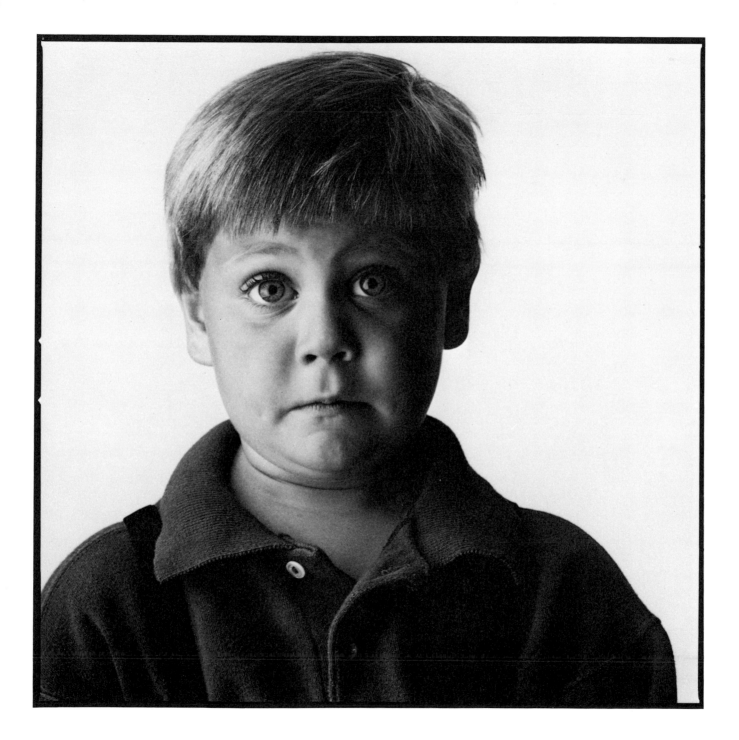

On Friday when I went to my cousin Janie's
she wouldn't let me play with her new dump truck
in the sandbox.

I always share my toys with her
when she comes to my house and I have something
new to play with.

I was…

Angry

On Saturday when I got up
my mother said it was a sunny day
so we could go to the playground
by the pond that has the ducks.

I went there once before
and played on this rope-climbing thing
that looked like a pirate ship.

I was...

Excited

On Sunday when I called my friend Peter
to see if he could come over to my house to play
his mother said he was sick.

My friend Kate couldn't play either
because she had to do errands with her big brother.

I was…

Lonely

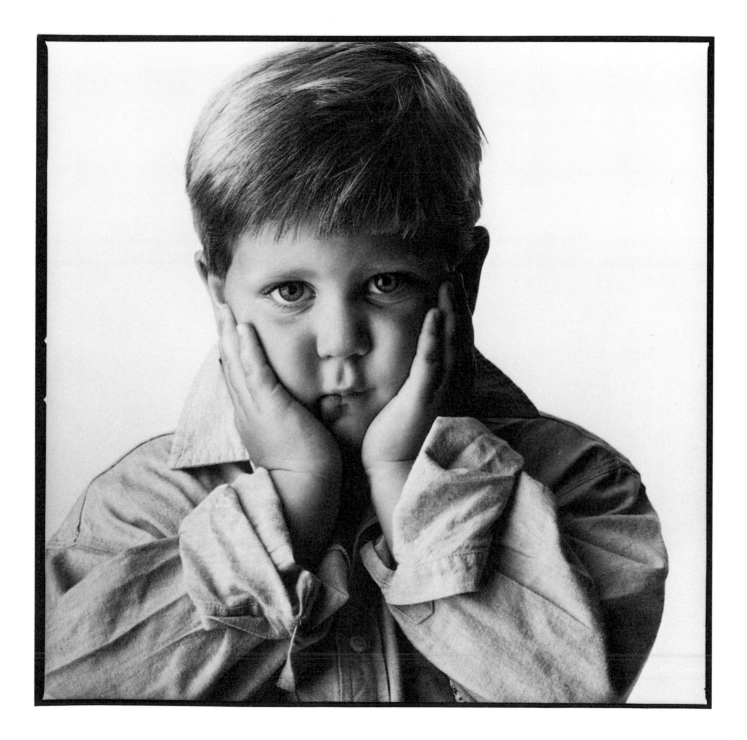

That night when my dad put me to bed
we started talking like we usually do.

I told my dad I thought
it had been quite a week
but my dad said he thought
most weeks are like that.

H-m-m-m…

I wonder.